Scary Mary

by Paula Bowles

Keep Out

tiger tales

This is
Scary Mary.

In the barnyard,
she ruled the roost.

If the other
animals
came near . . .

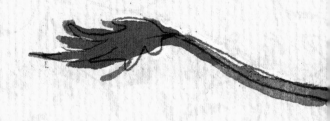

she chased them away!

She made signs,

and she put up gates,

and she
practiced

making

SCARY
faces.

She kept **all** the sunflower seeds to herself,

and **built** a fort to keep the others out.

sending
sunflowers
flying

and the animals
scurrying.

She **squawked**

and
clucked

and crowed,

and **flapped** her wings
in a terrific tantrum . . .

until

she

was

completely alone.

Finally
she had the
barnyard,

and everything in it,
all to herself.

She **clucked**
by herself,

played
by herself,

and
ate dinner
by herself.

But without
the others,

she soon
realized

that being scary . . .

was lonely.

So . . .

when the other animals were playing, Mary asked,

"Can I play, too?"

And they said . . .

Because it was much more
fun to do things . . .